T0142695

A 'Paws'itive Book
Dudley's
BIG Debut!!!

LJ.Bradfield

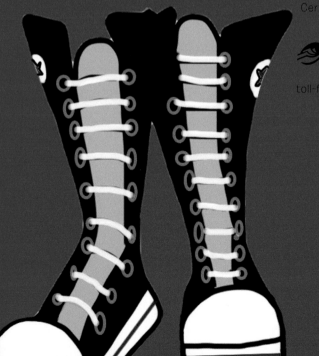

Dedicated to my beautiful niece

Ashlyn

Dudley wasn't big and Dudley wasn't strong,

but Dudley was a dog who could sing you a song.

He had a big dream of bright lights and a mic,

if only he didn't have nerves and stage fright.

He could jump through hoops and fly high like a kite

but singing on stage was just out of sight.

Dudley came from a family of Retrievers

and singing dogs didn't create many believers.

No one knew how well he could sing

and that one day he would be a rock and roll king.

Dogs chase rabbits and chase after cars.

Dogs don't sing rock and roll and play electric guitars.

But Dudley had rhythm and music inside,

something so special that no one should hide.

Sometimes when he spoke about singing on stage
the other dogs laughed and he crawled back in his cage.
They couldn't see the potential he had inside,
and that someday he'd be a canine of pride.

He practiced his guitar with rhythm and blues.

He even wore a pair of rock and roll shoes.

He sang in tune about songs of June

and dreamed that he'd be on the big stage soon.

Dudley believed that the day was near

when he would sing a song for everyone to hear.

So with his mind set on the sight

he got to work, for he had a song to write.

He stayed up late working hard on his song

he wanted it to be perfect, with nothing wrong.

For this was his chance and nobody knew

that this would be Dudley's BIG debut!!!

He set a plan for Friday night

and when everything was set up right

he held his guitar and grabbed the mic,

then stood up tall and shook off his stage fright.

He stood on the stage, right there in the park

and started to play alone in the dark.

Then the lights flicked on for everyone to see.

Dudley was singing with guitar, in key.

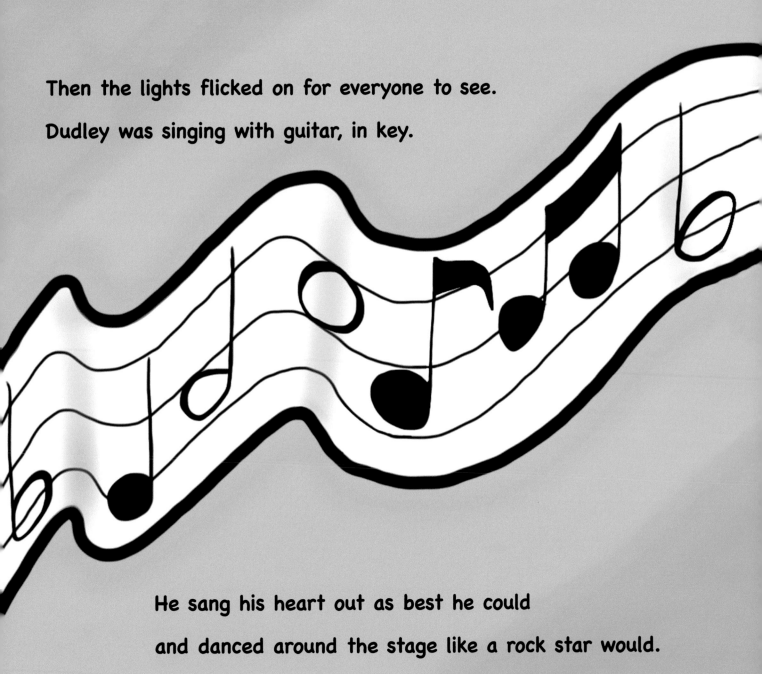

He sang his heart out as best he could

and danced around the stage like a rock star would.

His voice was loud - his voice was clear.

Finally he sang his song for everyone to hear.

The other dogs cheered and chanted his name,

from this moment on nothing would be the same.

Dudley was amazed that he had sung out loud

and that his friends and family were so proud.

It paid off big time to believe inside

that no one with a dream should ever hide.

For now everyone knew

this had been Dudley's BIG debut.

My Songs

_____

_____

_____

_____

_____

_____

_____

_____

_____

My Songs

_____

_____

_____

_____

_____

_____

_____

_____

_____

My Songs

_____

_____

_____

_____

_____

_____

_____

_____

_____

My Songs

_____

_____

_____

_____

_____

_____

_____

_____

_____

My Songs

_____

_____

_____

_____

_____

_____

_____

_____

_____

My Songs

_____

_____

_____

_____

_____

_____

_____

_____

_____

Printed in the United States
By Bookmasters